The mis-adventures of CASSIE

J.K. Palmer

F FREILING
PUBLISHING

Published by Freiling Publishing, a division of Freiling Agency, LLC.

70 Main Street, Suite 23-MEC
Warrenton, VA 20186

www.FreilingPublishing.com

Library of Congress Control Number: 2019906949

ISBN 9781950948062

Printed in the United States of America

What Real Kids Are Saying about
J.K. Palmer's
The Misadventures of Cassie

I think your stories are one of the best stories I've ever read. You are a great story writer! If you do decide to publish, I will buy every single one of your books.

— Kristin

All your stories were good! I liked every chapter. Are you going to write more stories?

— Mike

Thank you for sharing your stories with us. Your stories were excellent and very interesting too! When it was all done I wanted to read more and more.

— Jennifer

I thought all the stories you made were good. I liked the one when Cassie sneaked the cookies. Are you getting your stories published? I hope so, they are real good stories.

— Carrie

I thought your stories were creative. Thank you for writing them. I love your stories!

— Timothy

Dedication

This book is dedicated to all children of a certain age who are beginning to discover who they are, where they came from, and where they want to go next as they grow up and begin to find their own way. It is also dedicated to the people they can count on to be there for them, both family and friends, and those special teachers and mentors who care about children and nurture their natural curiosity and zest for learning and life.

And to my own inspirations: Linda, Debbie, Jim, David, Jeff, Tom, Tim, Andy, Jenn, Jill, Sue, Mike, Grace, Lucas, Jackson, Chloe, and Colin, with love.

Acknowledgments

"A journey of a thousand miles begins with
a single step" Laozi.

"The Misadventures of Cassie" began forty years ago
as a way to preserve my childhood memories for my
own children. I was helped by a class I took through
the University of New Hampshire in Concord taught by
N. M. Bodecker, himself a successful children's author.
He graciously agreed to personally edit and critique
my book and, along with the others in the class,
encouraged me to continue in my journey to have it
published.

Because he felt Cassie's stories were worth sharing
with others, I believed they were, too. In his summary
he had this to say:

"The characters and the neighborhood do come alive,
and for some reason it all seems to matter. I, for one
am glad to know that those people exist. It is gently
told, quite genuine, and quite un-selfconscious. What
this sort of book will mean to children I cannot tell,
though I should imagine that for many it would be
a welcome confirmation of their own lives." N. M.
Bodecker, 22nd Dec. 1982

Life has a way of getting in the way of our dreams
and aspirations with its pressing responsibilities and
detours, but I still want to thank him for his part in

this adventure. Even after all these years I took him at his word when time finally allowed me to "take up the pen" once again.

I also want to thank Thomas Freiling and Deborah Lewis of Freiling Publishing for their invaluable help and patience in navigating the publishing process. And a special thanks to my friend, Claudia Harbaugh, for her help in fine-tuning the manuscript and keeping my overuse of adverbs in check.

Table of Contents

Wandering

Cassie had been banished from the house. Not in disgrace; just as a matter of convenience for her mother. She had been getting into mischief all day long, and her mother's patience had just plain worn out.

The final straw came when Cassie decided that the perfect solution to all the commotion her little brothers were making was to stuff toilet paper in her ears so she could have some peace and quiet. It worked, but then she couldn't get the toilet paper out. It took her mother half an hour of poking in her ears before she finally pulled the last wadded-up ball of toilet paper out with tweezers. The first words Cassie heard clearly were, "Cassie Marie Johnson!" (the name her mother reserved for exasperating moments like this), "Go outside and play...NOW!"

It was the perfect time of year to be outside, and Cassie was pleased with her "punishment". She paused outside the door to pull up her socks, then decided to go barefoot and pulled them off instead. Leaving her shoes and socks on the back steps, she walked through the backyard towards The Field, and The Woods that lay beyond it.

Her mother's flower garden was in full bloom, and she stopped to check under the low-lying Sweet Williams for toads. She was about to give up her search when she spotted a good-sized one sitting quietly next to the chain link fence. She captured it with a quick swipe, but it peed on her as she cupped it in her hands. She squealed and adjusted her grip, wiping her hand on the grass as she did so.

Holding her squirming captive, she headed for the corner of the yard directly behind her father's small vegetable garden where her Toad Fortress was located. Built out of sticks, grass and clay it was where she kept toads while she was off searching for more toads. She didn't want to keep recapturing the same toad, and it was a challenge for her to see how many she could catch at any one time. Cassie deposited her first toad of the day in the Fortress, stayed long enough to be sure it couldn't jump high enough to escape, and then she climbed over the fence and into The Field.

All the houses on the block had fenced yards that bordered on the field. Many of the fences were covered with morning glory vines. Cassie loved to watch them close their petals in the late afternoon, but at the moment they were still open so she picked a few for a bouquet for her mother. As she continued walking through the open field she added some buttercups and Queen Anne's lace.

As she was bending over to pick some buttercups, she noticed an unusually lumpy patch of grass. Gently, she separated the grass to reveal the pink, hairless bodies of six baby field mice. Cassie was overjoyed! This was her best find yet! Sometimes, if she traveled two blocks to the field at the far end of their street, she could find some pheasant eggs, but never in her very own Field had she found such a treasure. She replaced the grass, then stood up to check her bearings. She was directly behind the Musslers' house, and just a few feet from The Pussy Willow Bush. Satisfied that she could relocate the nest to check on the mice again, she retrieved her bouquet and continued across The Field to enter The Woods.

The floor of The Woods was covered with moss, acorn caps, and nameless purple wild flowers. Normally, Cassie would gather the acorn caps for some project, or just count them to see how many she could find, but today she ignored them, only adding a few of the purple flowers to her bouquet before moving on. She only had one thought on her mind now. Butchie had been working on his fort at the far end of the clump of trees, and she wanted to spy on him.

Cassie's heart began to pound as she cautiously picked her way across the floor of The Woods, trying to avoid the noisy snap of a twig. As her heart raced, so did her imagination. She slipped from tree to tree, her mind alive with thoughts of what would happen to her if Butchie caught her spying on him.

Butchie was a legend with the neighborhood kids, and was feared by one and all. Even Cassie's parents would rather not tangle with Butch. He was the epitome of The Bad Kid; sassy, mean, disrespectful and a Real Bully. Tales abounded of children he had led in ropes to his Fort, making them eat all kinds of horrible things likes worms, creek water, and even poison ivy leaves! She had imagined herself being locked in The Fort so many times she was sure it had actually happened.

Spying on Butchie was considered one of the bravest things a neighborhood child could do, but Cassie did not feel brave at all when The Fort finally came into view. She noticed right away he had added a roof. She remembered, or at least she thought she remembered, sitting in The Fort, her hands tied behind her back, gazing at the trees above when there was no roof. She shuddered thinking about how much more dismal being captured would be now that there was a roof on The Fort. It would be dark, and scary. Cassie's stomach felt queasy at the thought, and she turned and fled back through The Woods, clutching her bouquet for dear life.

By the time she stopped running, she was back at the Toad Fortress. Her captive had escaped! Cassie frowned, forgetting about how scared she was of Butchie now that she was safely within view of her own house. She set about to recapture the toad.

"Maybe a roof on the Fortress would help" she thought as she wandered around The Field for a while, poking through the tall grass. With no toad in sight, she hopped the fence into her own backyard again and continued her search in the gardens. Still no luck. Finally, she gave up and made her way across the yard to the back steps where she deposited her wilting bouquet before heading down the driveway and across the street to The Pollywog Pond.

The Pollywog Pond was directly across from her house in the middle of a small meadow that was overgrown with out-of-season wild strawberries and crab grass. When the strawberries were in season, Cassie loved to pick them and pop them into her mouth; they were very small, but deliciously sweet.

One time her mother had asked her to pick enough for strawberry shortcake. It had taken her all afternoon to gather the tiny fruit, and even then, there was not enough for her mother to use. As she thought about it now, she realized Mrs. Johnson had come up with yet another creative way to get one of her children out of her hair for a few hours.

Cassie walked cautiously toward The Pollywog Pond, trying to avoid anything that might be hiding and could sting or poke her bare feet. When she safely reached the edge of The Pond she watched for several minutes as the pollywogs wiggled and darted away as she bent down, pretending she was going to catch them. She didn't have a jar with her, so she had to content herself with just watching instead of taking some home for an overnight visit on her dresser.

Part of the reason she had stayed away for a while was because Patrick, the boy she had a crush on, who lived on the next street over, had told her his brother had been bitten in half by a giant pinching beetle at The Pond. Even though Cassie laughed when Patrick told her his grisly and far-fetched tale, she secretly wondered if it could be true.

She was smiling to herself at how ridiculous it all sounded to her now, when her little sister, Christy, snuck up beside her and grabbed her arm.

"Christy!" Cassie exclaimed. "You scared me half to death! Go away!"

"Did you hear about Jackie Nudo's leg?" Christy replied, ignoring Cassie's command to leave.

"What about her leg?" Cassie asked, curious but still annoyed.

"Mama says she broke it today!" Christy explained.

"She broke her leg? Will it grow back?" Cassie asked.

"Grow back?" Christy responded, puzzled.

Cassie jumped up, grabbed Christy's hand, and pulled her toward the Nudo's house, which was directly next to the meadow. It was the fanciest house on the block, all brick with a porch in front and a birdbath in the yard. Jackie was an only child, and her mother was somewhat of a curiosity to Cassie. She had bleached blonde hair and no eyebrows, unless she penciled thin ones on for special occasions.

Cassie led Christy around to the back of the house, where, like little raccoons, they began to go through the garbage cans, looking for Jackie's broken leg. Just as they finished poking through the last can, they heard their mother calling them in for supper.

"Cassie Marie and Christine Joy, come home right now!" she called to the girls from the front door of the house. Abandoning their mission, they headed back across the street.

Cassie was the first one to face her mother in the front doorway. With her hands on her hips and her face set in a stern frown, Mrs. Johnson glared at her daughter.

"What do you think you were doing, going through the Nudos' trash cans?" she demanded.

"We were looking for Jackie's broken leg," Cassie replied, giving her mother a wink as she glanced back at Christy.

"You were what?!" Mrs. Johnson exclaimed, before bursting into laughter. "Wait until I tell your father this one! Oh, Cassie!" and she continued laughing as she turned into the house. "Come on, let's eat. Now. Both of you."

Christy looked at Cassie, perplexed, then followed her mother into the house. Cassie ran around to the back steps to retrieve her bouquet and shoes, and then she and her imagination went into the house to eat.

A Fish Story

Cassie's father was working second shift this week, and she could hardly contain herself. During the summer months, when school was out, it meant her father was home all day until 3:30 and they could do things together until he had to leave for work.

This particular day was especially exciting because Mr. Johnson had promised to take her fishing. Bounding out of bed, Cassie tiptoed down the stairs and knocked on her parents' bedroom door.

No one answered, so she cautiously opened the door and slipped around to her father's side of the bed where he was snoring steadily. She tapped him on his shoulder.

"Who is it," he said as he rubbed his eyes and squinted at Cassie. He couldn't see a thing without his glasses.

"It's me, daddy," Cassie whispered, "You promised to take me fishing today, remember?"

Her father mumbled and groped on the night stand for his glasses. Once he had them on, he took the alarm clock in his hand and pointed at it. "Cassie Marie, it's only 6:30. Now go back to bed and try me again at 8:00."

Cassie dragged herself back up the stairs and lay in bed, disappointed and wide awake. She had waited patiently for three weeks to hold her father to his fishing promise, and now she had to wait another hour and a half! It didn't seem fair.

When she finally heard her mother moving around in the kitchen below her, she quietly got dressed so she wouldn't wake Christy, and tiptoed, once again, down the stairs.

Her father was already at the table eating cornflakes, dressed in his fishing clothes. He had on his favorite grubby brown pants because he was so tall and thin he could never find jeans that fit properly. A faded blue shirt, worn golf cap, and his famous black and white sneakers completed his outfit. The sneakers were the same ones her father had worn when he played basketball in high school, and he was very proud they had survived all these years with only minor repairs and occasional new laces.

Cassie sat down across from him and they exchanged greetings and grins. She poured herself some Rice Krispies and forced them down, trying to chew each bite without letting them touch her tongue, and then tossing her head back so they could slide down her throat. She followed each bite with a quick gulp of orange juice. She hated Rice Krispies, but ever since her mother said she could send away for the international doll on the back of the box, she had been faithfully eating them every morning. So far, she had collected two box tops, and she only had to eat another half a box to get the third (and last) box top she needed.

By the time she had forced all her cereal down, Christy had joined them, as had her little brothers, Jeffrey and Tommy. Her older sister, Lenore, was still in bed, and probably would be for a while.

Cassie ignored them all and ran down the cellar stairs to get her homemade fishing pole and peanut butter jar of worms from behind the furnace where she had stashed them. She set them down outside the back door and peered through the screen door into the kitchen. She didn't dare bring the worms into the house; her mother had a "thing" about creepy, crawly things.

"I'm ready, daddy," Cassie announced.

Her father finished his coffee. "I'm coming! Let's go, Christy," he said as he headed toward Cassie. Christy finished her glass of orange juice and followed her father out the door.

Cassie couldn't believe her ears! Christy couldn't come! She'd ruin everything!

"I can't do anything without Christy," Cassie grumbled to herself. "Everything I do, she has to do, too. We always get the same things, go the same places, and have to share everything! This was supposed to be just me and daddy."

A scowl settled on Cassie's face as she grabbed her pole and stomped out to the car behind her father, who was holding Christy's hand. She knew better than to argue with him, so she silently got in the back seat and stared out the window while, in the front seat next to her father, Christy chattered away.

They drove about two miles to a secluded section of Cayuga Creek. Her father parked the car.

"Come on girls," he said cheerfully, ignoring Cassie's pouting.

After taking the gear out of the back of the car, he led the way through the tall grass toward the creek. His long legs easily overpowered the dense growth, but Cassie and Christy were struggling to keep up with him. After just a short distance, Christy started crying. Mr. Johnson walked back, scooped her up, and lifted her onto his shoulders.

Cassie continued, unassisted. She was glad she wasn't a "baby" like Christy, but sometimes she was jealous of the attention Christy's helplessness earned her. Gradually, she began to calm down, distracted by the damp grass grabbing at her legs.

It wasn't long before the grass gave way to a small grove of trees, and beyond the grove was The Fishing Spot. Mr. Johnson set Christy down on the stretch of grass that ran along the creek bed and handed both girls their fishing poles.

As he unscrewed the lid to the peanut butter jar that contained the worms, he winked at Cassie.

"Want to hook your own worm, Cassie?" he asked.

"Yuck!" she replied, sticking out her tongue and screwing up her face as she handed back her pole. There were some things in life Cassie had no desire to do herself; hooking worms was one of them.

After her father had baited her hook, the fishing ritual began. Cassie would toss her line out as far as it would go, wait a minute or two, then drag it in to check her bait. Christy, meanwhile, was getting more help from her father because every time she tried to toss her line into the water, the hook would catch on a branch, or a rock, or even Cassie! When her hook did manage to get into the water, it was usually only inches from the creekbank. Three times she caught Cassie's line and twice she caught reeds and her father had to cut her line and attach a new one.

After more than an hour of tangled lines and quiet waters, Christy began to get bored.

"Daddy, I wanna go home," she whined.

"Yeah, it doesn't look like we're going to get anything today. Let's go," her father replied.

Despite the fact they hadn't had a single nibble, Cassie was determined to stay until she caught a fish. "Please, dad, just a few more minutes?" she pleaded.

Her father thought a moment. "All right, just a few more minutes and then we're...Hey! Cassie! You've got a bite!"

Cassie yanked hard on the line as the bobber disappeared under the surface of the water. Her pole was bowed, and she found herself struggling to hold onto it.

Her father grabbed the pole from her.

"I can do it myself, dad," Cassie protested weakly.

"I don't think so, honey," he replied.

After a brief tug-of-war, he pulled the shiny, squirming fish from the creek and landed it on the grass. It jumped and flopped around as Cassie stared, her eyes wide and a goofy grin on her face.

"We got a fish; we got a fish!" Christy chanted as she jumped up and down.

Mr. Johnson cut the line after the fish settled down, put it in a large bucket, and handed it to Cassie. It was much too heavy for her to hold for long, so she quickly handed it back to her father. He lifted it easily, told the girls to gather up their gear, and then they headed to the car with Cassie's prize. Both girls got into the back seat and Mr. Johnson set the bucket on the floor between them.

"I'll stop for film on the way home so we can take a picture," her father said over his shoulder once the car was on the road.

They pulled into the shopping plaza parking lot and Mr. Johnson went into the drugstore to buy film. Cassie rolled down the window and leaned out, turning around occasionally to check on the fish as it flopped around in the bucket, and grinning broadly at complete strangers as they walked by. Christy wasn't sure she liked having a fish in the car with her, and was keeping her distance by squeezing up against the opposite door.

When their father returned, they headed for home; all three of them excited about how surprised the rest of the family would be.

They stopped at the corner market to have Mr. Wolney weigh the fish.

"Caught a carp, eh?" he asked Cassie as he examined the scales, "A big one, too. Three pounds and seven ounces," he announced in a booming voice.

Cassie and Christy looked at each other as their jaws dropped.

"WOW!" they said in unison.

When they pulled into the driveway, Mrs. Johnson, Lenore, and the boys all came out to admire the fish. Mr. Johnson took three pictures of Cassie holding the fish with Christy on one side and Tommy trying his best to get into the picture with them. It wasn't long before some of the neighbors wandered over to see what was going on, and they all complimented Cassie on her fine catch.

After the excitement finally died down, Cassie's father took her aside.

"We can't eat the fish, Cassie. It's a carp, and with all the garbage in the creek they just aren't safe to eat," he explained. "He's still alive. Why don't you put him in the creek down at the end of the street? Maybe he'll find his way back over to our fishing spot."

Cassie nodded. She hadn't wanted to eat the fish anyway. Now she understood why her father had been wetting the fish down.

For the first time, she noticed the fish's heaving gills. She'd better hurry or it was going to die!

She put the fish back in the bucket of shallow water and began to half carry, half drag it down the street toward the creek. She hadn't gone far when she put the bucket down, turned, and shouted at Christy.

"You coming or not, Christy?" she asked impatiently.

Christy's face lit up, and she ran to catch up with Cassie. Together they carried the bucket, stopping occasionally along the way to rest.

When they reached the creek, Cassie carefully tipped the bucket and slid the fish into the muddy waters. Together the girls waited anxiously to see if it would survive. A few minutes later it stopped heaving, flicked its tail, and disappeared into the murky, shallow waters.

Cassie turned away, relieved, and taking Christy's hand, she helped her climb the steep creek bank. When they reached the top, they headed home, the bucket still swinging between them as they chatted and bickered about the events of the day as only sisters can. Cassie decided she was glad Christy had come along on their fishing trip. Adventures, after all, are much more fun if someone is there to share them with you.

Cousins and Other Creatures

Mr. Johnson finished lashing the suitcases to the top of the station wagon and checked the knots one more time before he climbed into the driver's seat and rolled down the window. Cassie was sitting directly behind him with Lenore and an empty car seat for Tommy.

She was anxious to leave, but they had to wait for her mother while she took Tommy and Jeffrey to the bathroom "one more time just to be sure." It didn't take them long. She strapped Tommy into his car seat, then swung down the tailgate of the station wagon so Jeffrey could join Christy in the third-row seat which was stocked with an assortment of coloring books and small toys to keep them occupied on the long trip ahead. Mrs. Johnson settled into the front passenger seat, and rolled down her window. Finally, they could start their annual journey to visit her Aunt Phyllis and Uncle Art at their dairy farm in Ohio.

Cassie could hardly contain herself. It was an eight-hour trip to the farm, but worth every minute she had to endure sitting in the back seat with Tommy and Lenore. It was the only place they ever went on vacation, and the best part of her summer.

The farm was a magical place, inhabited by strange and wonderful creatures, from long-tongued cows to nervous chickens and shy barn cats. In addition to her stout aunt and chain-smoking uncle, an assortment of older, and somewhat unfriendly cousins lived in the sprawling farmhouse. Her Grandma Johnson had recently moved in, too. She was an oddly shaped woman, with long, flabby arms, hearing aids, false teeth, and straggly gray hair. She hardly ever smiled and rarely talked. Cassie was fascinated by each and every one of them.

Everything about the farm and her relatives was foreign to Cassie, especially the funny way they talked with their Ohio accent. It took a day or two for her to adjust to it so she could understand what they were saying, but by the end of each visit she sounded just like them, and kept the accent for a few days after they returned home. The week she spent there each summer was always an adventure.

Her father had driven the route to his boyhood home many times, and did not need a map. Even though it had been years since he had moved north away from the rural town in Ohio where he grew up, a part of him had never left.

The first leg of the drive was through the city of Buffalo and along Lake Erie. Cassie loved the stretch of road that took them up on The Skyway, a massive, tall expanse of bridge that ran along the shoreline of the lake. She could see for miles on a clear day. It always made her tummy flip-flop because it was like being on a roller coaster. They were so high up the ships out on the lake and the steel factories below looked like toys. She always worried they might drive off the side, but that was part of the reason she liked it so much.

After they left the city, the countryside began, and there wasn't much to see besides trees and fields, and more trees and fields, with an occasional farm or small town. They contented themselves with playing "I Spy" and "The Alphabet Game", reading books, coloring, or taking naps to make the time go by faster. About halfway there, Mr. Johnson announced that they were almost to Turkey Heaven. Everyone perked up and got ready for their first stop.

The only time the Johnsons ate restaurant food was when they got an occasional burger from the new McDonald's in town, Friday take-out fish fry dinners from Hanson's, and their yearly treat at Turkey Heaven. The restaurant was large and bright, with red and white checked table cloths and framed pictures of turkeys on the walls.

It took them a while to get settled, but soon they were feasting on generous helpings of turkey with stuffing, mashed potatoes and gravy, corn and butternut squash, with baskets of warm rolls and breads and an assortment of pies for dessert. They took a short stroll around the town square after they were done eating, and then piled back into the car to continue their journey.

Cassie slept for the next couple of hours, then tried to read her book. With Tommy asleep on her shoulder, she was cramped and sweaty in addition to being really bored. Just about then, The Hills began, and she knew they were getting closer to The Farm.

The roads through the foothills were narrow and winding, but Mr. Johnson knew them like the back of his hand, so he sped along at a good clip. From here on in, most of the scenery would be treetops with occasional glimpses of the surrounding hills. They passed a coal-mining area, with a huge mechanical shovel and dozens of dump trucks, and stopped briefly to watch them work so Mrs. Johnson could stretch her legs.

Soon after that they began to encounter a few tiny towns with old, broken down houses until, finally, they arrived at The Water Pump. Pulling the car off to the side of the road, everyone got out for their last stop before The Farm. Mrs. Johnson had brought paper cups along for the occasion, and they lined up to work the pump and catch the cold, pure spring water that sloshed out. Refreshed and eager with anticipation, they only had to round a couple more curves before pulling into the steep dirt driveway that ran next to the farmhouse and beyond it to the back pasture.

As they piled out of the car, familiar farm smells filled Cassie's nostrils as she ran up to the wrap-around porch where her aunt and grandmother were waiting. After hugs and greetings all around, Mr. Johnson began to unload the roof rack and distribute suitcases to take into the house.

Cassie and Christy took turns dragging their suitcase up the narrow stairs to the bedroom they would share with their cousins for the next week. The large sleeping area consisted of two long, narrow rooms with a doorway in between, with double beds lining the walls on one side and dressers on the other. Her six girl cousins shared this space, while her cousin Jimmy had a small room off the downstairs parlor. When they came to visit, Cassie and her siblings slept wherever they could find a space, but usually she was able to find a spot on a real bed.

Her cousins hardly noticed she was there. They were boisterous and busy and older than she was, most of them by several years, so she observed them more than anything else. Like a fly on the wall, she listened in on their conversations about boyfriends, dates, dances, and gossip, drinking in every word and curious about a life that was so different from her own.

The chaos at home was nothing compared to having sixteen people living under one roof. Most of the rooms were spacious and sparsely furnished, with bare wood floors and scatter rugs, so there was plenty of room to spread out, but there was only one bathroom, plus an outhouse for emergencies.

Cassie liked the fact that even going to the bathroom was an adventure. If she woke up in the middle of the night and had to use the bathroom, a flashlight was hanging by the back door just in case the inside john was occupied and she couldn't wait. She'd trek across the backyard to the outhouse, which was not too far from the chicken coop, in total darkness and eerie silence. Each time she slammed the door behind her, going in and coming out, the chickens would momentarily put up a fuss, and then it would be silent again.

Grandma Johnson and Aunt Phyllis served up a huge breakfast every morning. Uncle Art would bring in a basket of eggs and a bucket of fresh milk from the barn, and they would make eggs-to-order plus cook up pancakes and bacon or hot muffins. Everyone ate in shifts around two big tables in the large kitchen.

Afterwards, her cousins all had chores to do or jobs to go to, so by mid-morning every day Cassie was free to poke around on her own to find something interesting to explore. Most of the time, she tagged along with her Uncle Art as he worked around the farm since her aunt and grandmother were busy preparing meals and tending to household chores while her mother took it easy.

Mrs. Johnson was going to have another baby soon, so she was not allowed to lift a finger other than keeping an eye on Tommy and Jeffrey. This was her vacation, too. Mr. Johnson spent most of his time sitting in the kitchen reminiscing with his sister or taking short jaunts to visit his old haunts to spend time with his friends from high school.

Uncle Art was a quiet man, and while Cassie tailed him, he rarely said a word to her. After a couple days, she tired of simply watching him work, and decided to venture out on her own. She started her hike in the meadow closest to the farmhouse.

The upper pasture there was fenced, but she was able to climb through the large swinging gate. Once on the other side, she went directly to the fast running stream that fed The Water Pump with its crystal-clear water. She could see crawdaddies running along the stones on the bottom. She had been crawdad hunting there once before with her cousin Faith, and knew her father would be proud of her for catching one, so she plunged her hand into the ice-cold water and promptly was pinched by a crawdad!

Startled, she jumped up, and fell backwards onto an old cow patty. Picking herself up, she found a patch of clover nearby, sat down, and wiped her back end off as best she could. Her finger wasn't bleeding, but she decided to go back through the gate to the farmhouse to change her clothes.

As she headed toward the house, standing in the pasture, between her and the gate, was a herd of cows Uncle Art had led up from the barn for their midday grazing. He was nowhere in sight.

Cassie was terrified of cows. They were huge, smelly creatures, with long sticky tongues, their bodies covered with flies that they flicked with their whip-like tails while they stared at her with spooky, protruding eyes. She was sure they were either going to lick her, flick her, or step on her toes with their sharp hooves.

She had to get back to the farmhouse, but the only way she knew of to get there was blocked. Then, off to her left, behind the chicken coop, she spotted a tree she could climb to get over the fence and into the back yard. She made a dash around the cows for the tree, and in the process tripped over one of the many small rocks that dotted the meadow, fell into a clover patch and felt a sharp pain in her knee. She had landed on a bumble bee! She watched in disbelief as her knee began to swell and throb.

Scrambling to her feet once again, she kept running toward the tree. She shinnied up the trunk and inched her way out onto the branch that extended over the fence, then swung down and dropped onto the ground behind the chicken coop. Immediately, dozens of chickens swarmed around her, curious to see if she had any feed for them. They followed her as she crept along the low fence that surrounded the coop until she found the gate, her sneakers now covered in chicken poop, her finger sore and her knee continuing to swell.

She pushed the latch on the gate and backed out, catching her shorts pocket on a protruding nail, ripping the seam and gashing her leg.

Bursting into tears, she ran the last few yards to the house, stumbled up the steps onto the back porch and then limped through the screen door into the kitchen.

Cassie was looking for help, and some sympathy, but she was greeted with dropped jaws and gales of laughter instead. Within minutes the whole family had gathered in the kitchen to take a look at Cassie and chuckle at her sorry state. Her cousin, Shirley, had just offered to take her to the bathroom to clean up, when Uncle Art came storming through the door.

"Who let the chickens out?" he hollered.

Sure enough, Cassie had neglected to latch the gate behind her and the chickens were wandering all over the yard, up on the porch, and even into the road. Uncle Art was fuming mad, Cassie was embarrassed, but everyone else was having a grand time laughing at her predicament. While Cassie washed up, her cousins helped their father round up the chickens.

Her messy misadventure was a turning point for Cassie with her cousins. They seemed to notice her for the first time, and took her under their wing. They spent their evenings together, sitting on the roof outside the bedroom window telling tall tales and jokes, or on the wrap-around front porch watching the big trucks go by. Faith and Pam took her with them into Wheeling to swim at the public pool there, and one night they walked up the road and around the bend to the ice cream parlor she never knew was there before.

They played pick-up sticks on the hardwood floor in the parlor, and took her fishing for sunfish in the pond next to the barn. Jimmy even took her for a tractor ride, and let her help him gather eggs. But best of all, they showed her where the barn cats and a litter of kittens were hiding in the hay in the loft.

On their last day there, her cousin Judy gave her one of her high school pictures with a message on the back. She promised she would write to her. Cassie tucked it into her suitcase along with her other mementos from her best vacation yet.

Before they got into the car for their long journey home, everyone gathered for final photos of the families together. Cassie made a quick trip to the barn, and returned with one of the kittens in her arms. Standing with her brothers and sisters, she held the kitten up, a big grin on her face, while her father and Uncle Art snapped pictures with their cameras.

All of a sudden, her grandmother came charging towards her, plucked the kitten from her hands, and held it at arms' length as she hobbled back towards the barn.

"This thing has fleas AND lice," she hollered back over her shoulder. "It belongs in the barn!"

Mrs. Johnson handed Tommy over to Lenore, and marched Cassie into the house to wash her hands. Cassie felt itchy all over as she thought about the hours she had spent playing in the hay with the kittens. This was one vacation she would never forget, she mused to herself as she scratched her head. And then she had the satisfying thought that neither would anyone else.

Four Eyes

It was the last day of summer vacation and Cassie was excited to be going back to school the next day. She knew her new teacher's name, and her room number, but she had no idea if any of her classmates from last year would be in the same class. It didn't really matter much to her either way because she loved school because it was school, and who she shared a classroom with made no difference to her. She had plenty of time to play when she got home.

The first day of school was always special, which was why, the week before, Mrs. Johnson had taken her shopping to make sure she was ready for it with a new outfit and shoes to match. Most of her clothes were hand-me-downs from older cousins, which is why Cassie was so proud of the new blue dress that was ironed and hung up on her closet door.

Something else was new this year for Cassie. She was about to get her first pair of glasses.

"Cassie," her mother yelled out the front door as Cassie was playing hopscotch on the front sidewalk. "It's time to go! Come on!"

Dragging her feet more than a little, Cassie went inside, ran a brush through her hair, washed her hands, and looked at her plain old face in the mirror one last time before heading out to the car.

When she opened the back door to slide in, she discovered the whole family was in the car, and the only spot left for her was in the way-back third seat of the station wagon with Christy. The seat faced backwards and the view was boring, but she had no choice, so she swung down the tailgate and climbed in next to her sister.

Her father made sure they were settled in and the tailgate was secure before getting into the driver's seat and pulling out of the driveway to head to the optometrist's office.

It had been a week since Cassie had first walked into Dr. Hayes' office and she was not looking forward to going back. But then it dawned on her! He had a stack of Highlights magazines in the office! She could read the stories and find the hidden objects while they waited, like she had last time.

Dr. Hayes' office was downtown so it took them a while to get there. When they arrived, Mr. Johnson parked the car out front and Mrs. Johnson came around to the back of the car, dropped the tailgate, and Cassie scrambled out, following her mother into the darkly lit office. Everyone else stayed in the car, the motor running and windows down.

Mrs. Johnson signed in, then slowly lowered herself and her obvious baby bump into a chair next to Cassie, whose head was already buried in a Highlights magazine.

"Don't get too wrapped up in that magazine, Cassie. This should only take a few minutes," her mother advised. Sure enough, the door to the waiting room opened, and Dr. Hayes himself was standing there.

"Cassie Johnson?" he asked, looking straight at her.

Mrs. Johnson pushed herself up and out of her chair, motioned for Cassie to do the same, and together they followed Dr. Hayes down the hall to the small fitting room they had used the week before to pick out the frames for her new glasses.

"Sit down right here, young lady," he said, pointing to the chair opposite his at the narrow fitting table. "Hello, Mrs. Johnson," he continued as he pulled a pair of glasses out of a pretty brocade case, sprayed and polished them, and sat down across from her and her mother. "Let's see how these glasses fit and what you think of them, Cassie. You picked out quite a nice frame."

Cassie shifted in her chair to get closer as he slid the glasses over her ears and settled them on her nose. Then he sat back to watch her reaction as she turned toward the mirror to see the pale blue cat-eye frames she had picked out, all by herself.

"Don 't they look sharp," her mother finally said. Cassie kept staring at herself without saying a word, trying to get used to the strange new face in the mirror.

When she finally turned away to glance at her mother, she caught a glimpse of a framed sign on the wall that she hadn't noticed before. She could see every word clearly, and began to read it out loud, "The Small Western Optical College, Kansas City, Missouri, Diploma, Walter Eugene Hayes, Doctor of Optometry."

Her eyes shifted to the neat rows of frames that lined the walls, then to the ceiling tiles above her head, and finally to the clock on the wall. It was 10:05. In five short minutes her life had completely changed.

As her mother and Dr. Hayes shook hands and made small talk, Cassie continued to look around. She barely heard Dr. Hayes' parting words. "It will take a couple of days for your eyes to adjust because you have quite a bit of astigmatism, so things will be a little distorted. But once your brain gets used to seeing properly, you'll be just fine."

Mrs. Johnson paid the bill and headed toward the door, but Cassie raced ahead of her. She pulled open the door to see her father and brothers and sisters hanging out the windows of the car, craning to see her new glasses.

She paused in the doorway, grinned, and shouted, "I can see!" then misjudged the step down to the sidewalk, tripped over her own feet, and fell face-first, landing on her hands and knees.

Everyone started laughing except Mrs. Johnson, who glowered at them before helping Cassie to her feet and making sure she was all right. Cassie climbed into the back seat, her knees a bit scraped up and slightly embarrassed, but thrilled she could see so much better.

Later that night, lying in bed, Cassie stared around her at the details she had never noticed before because she could not see them.

From the cobwebs in the corners, and the thin layer of dust on her dresser, to the gentle folds and swiss dots on the curtains that framed the tiny window, everything was sharp, clear, and fascinating. Reluctantly, she finally took off her new glasses, tucked them in their brocade case, put them on the nightstand, and switched off the lamp next to her bed. It had been a good day.

The next morning Cassie and Christy headed out the door for school, both wearing new dresses and shoes. Cassie's glasses were perched on her nose, but she still wasn't completely used to them, so the ground seemed closer than it was. She had to watch her step. With her head down to make sure she didn't trip again, no one seemed to notice she was wearing glasses until they arrived at the school and got in line, waiting for the doors to open.

As she was looking around, checking out who was there, without warning, a boy Cassie did not even know turned around and began taunting her.

"Four eyes, four eyes," he started chanting. The boy continued teasing her and a few of his friends joined in. "Four eyes, four eyes!"

Cassie glared at the boy, trying to decide what to do, but just then the principal swung open the door and the long line of students rushed forward to find their way to their new classrooms. The boy and his friends disappeared into the crowd.

Cassie helped Christy find her classroom, then hurried down the hallway to her own, still fuming over being called Four Eyes. It had never occurred to her that anyone would even notice her new glasses. She didn't think anyone noticed her at all!

As she took her seat at the desk with her name on it, she glanced around the room to see if she knew anyone from last year's class and was happy to see a few friends, including Emily Holstein who also wore glasses, way at the back of the room. Emily waved at her and grinned, pointing at her own glasses, then Cassie's, and nodding her approval.

Cassie grinned back, then turned around to face the blackboard where she saw her new teacher's name written on it. "Miss Edie" it read, in bold, white chalk. She couldn't believe her eyes! She could see so much better with her new glasses.

Cassie decided right then and there that being called Four Eyes was not an insult after all. She would not let anything, or anyone, take away the happiness she felt being able to see the blackboard, and everything else she had been missing. Seeing clearly was worth all the silly teasing in the world.

The Fateful Day

There were a lot of things that displeased Cassie: like when her mother said "no", or when she had to share things, or when she was sent to bed when it was still light out and the other kids were playing right outside her window. But there were really only two things she hated: one was not being The Best at something, and the other was being told she couldn't do something because she was A Girl. Occasionally those two most hated things happened at the same time as she fought her own private battle against becoming Ordinary.

Cassie tried her hardest to be The Best in everything she did. She was the loudest one at the dinner table in order to be heard. But she was the quietest one in class in order to be praised. She was super polite in public in order to get the good type of attention rather than the bad type. She did her best to run the fastest, jump the furthest, burp the loudest, and be the right-est. She wanted people to think she was witty, talented, well-behaved, and cute. Anything but Ordinary.

Cassie also tried her best to ignore the fact that she was A Girl. She viewed it more as an inconvenience than a major problem, but it still annoyed her that it made people treat her differently.

It had never bothered her to be a girl until the past summer when her father told her she was getting older and had to wear a shirt all the time now because she was a girl. Then her mother began to lecture her on sitting properly, and behaving like A Lady.

Cassie just wanted to be Cassie, so she fought back by bragging about not being afraid of bugs (with the exception of big, hairy spiders), took to spitting occasionally, refused to wear a dress when she didn't have to, and teased Christy and her friends who spent most of their time playing with dolls. She even made a solemn vow to herself to never, ever, carry a purse.

There were times Cassie secretly enjoyed some aspects of being a girl. She liked having a boyfriend, or two, and once in a while imagined herself as a beautiful princess, but she would never admit it. Sometimes, in her attempts to not be a sissy, she even did things she didn't like, or were just plain dumb. But she enjoyed being the neighborhood tomboy and The Best so much that she was willing to do just about anything to protect her reputation.

On The Fateful Day, Cassie's two worst fears came together in the worst way. By the end of the day, she had to accept that she wasn't The Best at everything, and that being a tomboy could be hazardous to your health.

Cassie had been working all week on a big project for school. It was a book of poems that she had written, complete with illustrations. There were ten poems in all, but her two favorite ones were about her younger sister Christy's freckles and missing teeth:

Freckle-Faced You
Freckle-faced you,
With so many things to do,
Little dots all o'er your face,
Like the stars all up in space.

Toothless Annie
Toothless Annie, that is you!
Pull your teeth is what you do.
Every month you pull one out
Until you can't even shout.

When she read the poems to her family at the dinner table the night before they were due, everyone smiled. Lenore even laughed, which made Cassie more confident than ever. She just KNEW her poems would be The Best in the class.

After dinner her father announced he was getting a new jack knife the next day. His old one was dull and chipped, and the handle was cracked. Cassie could hardly contain her excitement. When she was done helping with the dishes, she mustered up enough courage to approach her father to ask him for his old knife. To her, a jack knife was a true symbol of manhood. Her father whittled with his, cleaned his nails, picked his teeth, and seemed to be able to fix just about anything. She didn't know what she would do with an old jack knife, but she wanted it in the worst way.

She begged and pleaded until she wore her father down. He agreed to at least talk to her mother about letting her have his old knife the next day. Cassie was ecstatic. She didn't know a single girl, and only a few boys, who possessed such a Treasure.

When the Fateful Day arrived the next morning, Cassie couldn't wait to get to school. She sailed into class and waited smugly for her turn to read her poems and bask in her moment of glory.

But something went wrong. Just before it was her turn to read her poems, Joyce Kosnick read her poem, and Cassie's heart sank. Joyce's poem was really good; her poem was better than Cassie's; her poem was The Best.

When Joyce was done, Cassie walked to the front of the room and read her poems with little enthusiasm. No one was paying attention. Everyone was still chuckling over Joyce's poem.

When she got home, she immediately went to find her mother who was folding laundry on the living room couch. "Mama," she asked, "would you like to hear my new poem?"

"Sure, Cassie," her mother replied.

So, Cassie recited Joyce's poem as if it were her own:

> Susie has a little car,
> The little car is red.
> And everywhere that Susie goes,
> People are falling dead.

Cassie's mother smiled and hugged her. "That's your best one yet, honey", she said.

Cassie just nodded and went to her room.

At the dinner table that night, Cassie recited her new poem for the entire family. Lenore rolled her eyes, Christy and her father thought it was great, and Jeffrey and Tommy didn't get it at all. Cassie didn't care. They were too young to enjoy grade school humor.

It was Lenore's turn to help with dishes, so her father took Cassie aside right after supper. He slipped something cold and hard into her hand. It was his old knife. She barely heard her father as he laid out the rules for the knife.

"I got my new knife today, Cassie," he said. "Your mother and I have decided to let you have my old one on a trial basis, but she's not happy about it. It stays in the house, don't even think about using it without supervision, and we need to talk about the safe way to handle it. If you misuse it, you lose it. Hey! That rhymes – kind of like your poems. By the way, I really liked that new one – very funny. Now give me a few minutes to read the paper and then I'll give you a lesson on how to handle a jack knife."

As her father wandered into the living room to read the newspaper, Cassie stared down at the old knife with its cracked, mottled handle and thick, dull blade. Without a word, she ran out the side door and headed for The Woods with her new possession. She went straight to her favorite climbing tree, then up its trunk to perch in the crook where she could examine it more closely. She had no intention of actually using the knife. It was simply something she could brag about, and a connection to her father. Then, without really thinking, she gave in to a girlish whim and carved her initials and those of Patrick Shaw into the thick bark.

Just as she finished the "S", the blade broke and the knife slipped, slashing the knuckle of her middle finger. Blood began to gush out of the deep gash, but she was so surprised, and so immediately concerned about getting into trouble, that she didn't even cry. Instead, she silently clambered down the tree and ran toward the house, squeezing her finger tightly to slow the bleeding.

Her mother was sitting on the steps watching the boys play when Cassie approached her. She tried to hide her hand behind her back, hoping to slip into the house to find a band aid, but she could feel the blood dripping off the end of her finger onto the ground, and the sight of her mother made her lower lip tremble and tears well up in her eyes.

"Cassie, what's wrong?" her mother asked.

"I cut my finger," Cassie replied, her voice beginning to break.

"How'd you do that?" her mother asked suspiciously.

Cassie's mind whirled, groping for an explanation that would get her, and her father, out of trouble. "It was Butchie and Larry Jones, ma," she blurted out. "They took me, and made me stand in front of a tree, and Larry held my hand while Butchie took a knife and threw it at me and cut my knuckle!"

Her mother gasped as Cassie pulled her bloody hand from behind her back and held it out for her to see. She immediately pinched the wound shut with one hand while she pushed Cassie into the house with the other to determine if she needed stitches. She cleaned and bandaged the ugly cut, fashioned a splint with a popsicle stick and decided a trip to the emergency room wasn't necessary, at least for now.

As she worked on Cassie's finger, she didn't say anything about Cassie's outrageous story. She did mutter "Why can't you play with dolls like all the other little girls?" and then she sent Cassie to bed early so she could talk to her father, alone.

Cassie lay in bed, asking herself the same question. She wasn't pleased at all with the day's events, or with herself for lying. For the first time she was almost ready to be an ordinary girl. She pulled the covers up over her head so she couldn't hear the other children playing outside, her throbbing finger the focus of her attention. Then suddenly she had a thought: "Boy," she smiled to herself. "I sure will have a story to tell at school tomorrow. It will be the Best One yet!"

Out of Sorts

"Nothing ever goes my way! Nobody understands!"
Cassie yelled at her mother as she slammed the door to
the cellar and raced down the wooden stairs.

"Cassandra Marie," her mother shouted after her, as
she opened the door and stood at the top of the stairs
with her hands on her hips. "Get back up here right
now. You KNOW you aren't supposed to hit your little
brother!"

There was silence from Cassie.

"All right," her mother finally said. "Stay down there
until you've cooled off, and then we're having a little
talk, young lady!" then she closed the door, leaving
Cassie alone in the cool, dark cellar.

Cassie crouched in the walk-thru behind the furnace;
hot, angry tears welling up in her eyes. Her whole
body was clenched, but she relaxed slowly as the tears
began to run down her cheeks and drip off her chin.

After a few minutes, she calmed down enough to make her way over to the washing machine where she found a damp towel on top of one of the mounds of dirty clothes that surrounded it. After sniffing it to be sure it wasn't too gross, she wiped her face and blew her nose and threw it back on top of the pile.

"It's all Jeffrey's fault," she muttered to herself. "He's always wrecking my things. And all Ma ever says is 'He's just a little boy. He doesn't know any better!' Ha! Sure he does!"

Suddenly remembering something, she pulled the cord to turn on the overhead light and peered cautiously under the cellar stairs into the trash can that was kept there. She was relieved when she saw her doll, Petunia, was gone. Just some old boxes and paper trash were there now, along with their cat, Puffy's, litter box.

Cassie hadn't played with Petunia often, but she had been her favorite doll.

The week before, Christy had decided to play with Petunia without Cassie's permission, and that was when the "accident" happened.

She was playing with Petunia and two of her own dolls, Rhoda and Gracie, on the top bunk in the boys' bedroom. Jeffrey was playing on the floor next to the bunk beds when Petunia fell to the floor, right in the middle of his toy soldiers. Grabbing the doll, he jumped onto the lower bunk and squeezed into the corner next to the wall while Christy leaned over the edge of the top bunk trying to reach him and Petunia.

Jeffrey kept poking the doll at Christy's flailing hands and then snatching it away just as she almost grabbed it. Finally, Christy managed to latch on to Petunia's head and she and Jeffrey began a tug-o-war, giggling and shrieking until poor Petunia's head popped off.

Just the thought of her poor doll losing her head made Cassie mad at Jeffrey all over again.

"That kid is always ruining everything," she fumed. "First he killed the guppy I bought with my own money by dumping a whole box of fish food in the bowl, then he wrecked my favorite doll, and now he's stolen my favorite rock from my rock collection and won't 'fess up." She kicked the washtub leg, stubbed her toe, and fell against the metal shelves where Mrs. Johnson kept her laundry supplies.

Tucked behind the bleach was the shoebox that contained Cassie's Experiments, and she almost knocked them off before she was able to steady the shelving unit. Carefully, she took down the box and removed the lid to make sure they were okay.

Inside the shoebox were ten baby food jars, each with a different combination of ingredients. One jar had laundry soap and grass with water in it. Another had pepper, vinegar, and bleach. One even had a dead fly with applesauce and oregano. She checked each one for any changes that may have occurred since the last time she looked at them. She was pleased to note that one had fuzzy green mold all over it, but the others were pretty much the same as they were when she put them together the week before.

"He's just a little boy," Cassie muttered to herself, mimicking her mother's tone of voice. "Next thing you know he'll probably wreck my Experiments, too."

With that thought in mind, she stood on her tiptoes and slid the shoebox onto the highest shelf, out of Jeffrey's reach, just as her mother opened the door to the cellar again.

"Cassie, it's time to go to Pioneer Girls Club. Are you going, or do you plan on spending the rest of the evening in the cellar?" she asked.

"I'm coming," Cassie said as the bounded up the stairs. Her gray mood lifted instantly at the thought of going to her beloved Pioneer Girls Club.

By the time Cassie retrieved her badge book and Bible from her dresser, her mother was waiting in the car and Cassie had almost forgotten about Jeffrey. Still, she wasn't sure if her mother had forgiven her behavior, so she got in the back seat of the station wagon and waited silently to see if her mother said anything.

Without a word her mother put the car in reverse and glanced at Cassie as she started to back out of the driveway. Just as the car began to move, there was a sudden THUMP! and then a loud "MEOWR!" as the family cat, Puffy, streaked up the driveway and disappeared behind the house.

"Oh, for pity's sake, I've hit the cat," Cassie's mother exclaimed as she jammed the car into park and eased herself out from behind the steering wheel to walk as fast as she could after the cat.

Their neighbor, Mr. Young, who had been mowing his lawn and saw what had happened, ran after Mrs. Johnson, just as her father flew out the front door and followed them both around to the back of the house. Cassie sat frozen in the back seat of the car.

When her mother finally emerged, alone, from the back yard, Cassie knew what had happened. Terror welled up inside her, and she began to cry uncontrollably. When she opened the door and tried to go to the back yard to see Puffy, her mother blocked her and pulled her into a hug.

"You can't go back there, Cassie," she said gently. "Now, come on, let's go to Pioneer Girls."

Cassie glared at her mother in disbelief. How could she go to club after what had just happened to her cat?

"I can't go, Ma," Cassie wailed.

"Yes, you can, honey. Now get in the car, Cassie. It won't do you any good to stay home," her mother said firmly.

Cassie cried off and on all the way to the church while her mother tried to explain to her what had happened.

"She must have been sleeping on top of the tire. I always check behind the car before I back up. I'm so sorry, hon, but I'm sure she didn't suffer much," she said in her last effort to console Cassie. By the time they arrived at the church, Cassie had stopped crying, but her eyes were red and swollen.

During club her friends and the leaders kept asking her why she was so upset. It wasn't until the end of the meeting before she could finally tell them about her terrible day. She felt better when she saw the concern and sympathy on their faces. Taking her hand on either side, the group formed a circle and prayed for her and Puffy. Each of her friends gave her a hug before they left, and Cassie was glad she had come.

On the way home, Cassie's mother let her sit in the front seat. She stared silently out the side window, her back to her mother, wondering where they had buried Puffy. Her mother finally broke the silence.

"You know Cassie," she began, "when you were a little girl you would come to me whenever you got a booboo, and I'd kiss it and make it all better. But one day when I kissed your booboo, I could tell it still hurt. From the look on your face I knew I had lost my magical powers that day. I felt so bad, because I couldn't make your booboos stop hurting anymore."

Cassie ventured a look in her mother's direction. She wasn't sure exactly what her mom was trying to tell her, but she felt for the first time that day that maybe her mother did understand after all.

When they drove into the driveway and came to a stop, Cassie waited for her mother to come around to the passenger side and open the door for her. Mrs. Johnson kissed the top of Cassie's aching, weary head as she rested it on her mother's arm and they walked, hand in hand, up the steps and into the house.

My House, My Friend

Cassie was home sick from school with the flu. She had already missed two days and was feeling just well enough to be bored and restless, but not well enough to go back to school, or so she had convinced her mother.

"Cassie," Mrs. Johnson yelled from the kitchen.

"Yes, mama," Cassie replied in her best sick-sounding voice.

"Come here, child. I can't hear you," her mother shouted back impatiently.

Pulling her bare feet out from under her cozy afghan, Cassie laid her book face down on the pillow to save her place, and slowly made her way into the kitchen.

Her mother and two little brothers, Jeffrey and Tommy, were standing by the back door, obviously ready to leave. Mrs. Johnson had Tommy perched on her pregnant belly, and Jeffrey was carrying her purse.

"What, mama," Cassie said weakly.

"I have to go to the store for a few things. You're getting to be a pretty big girl. Do you think I can leave you home alone for a little while?" her mother asked.

Cassie nodded, trying her best to hide her excitement.

"Mrs. Young is home if you need her. Her number's right next to the phone. Just stay in the house, and stay out of trouble. We won't be long," and she disappeared out the door with the boys.

Cassie watched out the picture window in the living room as the car pulled out and drove away. As soon as it was out of sight, she began to giggle and dance around the coffee table with glee.

"I'm alone," she crowed. "Just me, and The House."

Cassie had never thought much about her house before. It was just "there". Now, all alone in it, she felt very secure. It was a warm house, simple and familiar. Being alone in "her" house wasn't scary at all, she decided.

Then it dawned on her; this was her chance to go exploring!

She stopped dancing around and plopped into her father's chair. She NEVER got to sit there when he was home, and if he wasn't home, she had to fight for a turn with her brothers and sisters. She felt her father's presence as she burrowed into the overstuffed cushions. It was almost as satisfying as having him all to herself for a few precious moments.

She sat there for quite a while, planning her strategy for exploration, then slid out of the chair and headed for her first stop; the kitchen. She counted the number of steps it took to get to the cookie jar. Fourteen giant steps. She peeked inside. There were two Oreos left, and a handful of crumbs.

"She'll notice for sure if I take the last two cookies," she thought to herself. But she took them anyway, poured herself a glass of milk, and sat down at the table.

The table seemed so quiet, and big. As she relished her milk-soaked cookies, she stretched out her elbows then wiggled and kicked her feet in all directions. No one kicked back! No one yelled at her for having her elbows on the table or for dunking her cookies in her milk.

When a piece of Oreo broke off, she thrust her whole hand into the glass, fished out the soggy remains, and popped them into her mouth.

Finished with her snack, she rinsed out the glass so her mother wouldn't see all the crumbs in the bottom, then went to the bathroom to check her face for "evidence" and wash her sticky hands.

"Hello there, you gorgeous thing," she crooned as she fluffed her hair and posed dramatically for the mirror as she sat on the edge of the sink. She finished washing up, pushed her glasses back up on her nose, then made her best "ugly face" by crossing her eyes, sucking in her nostrils, and sticking out her tongue and curling it up to make a big, fat, upper lip.

When she was done primping and giggling at herself, she ventured across the hall to her parents' room. Cassie opened the door and stood for a long time in the doorway. She could feel her heart pounding and a guilty flush creeping over her face. This was forbidden territory; the one place in the house where no children were allowed without their parents' permission.

The room was dark because the shades were pulled, but she could tell it was crowded with furniture and cluttered with the many "projects" her mother was working on. Even the crib for the new baby was nestled in one corner, so there was barely room to move around.

Cassie switched on the light, debating whether or not to trespass. Curiosity finally got the best of her, and she walked cautiously toward the dresser her parents shared, only one goal in mind.

There it was! Her father's wooden jewelry box with the picture of the handsome clipper ship sailing across the lid. Butterflies playing in her stomach, she lifted the lid and tenderly fingered the odds and ends inside. One by one she examined them: cuff links, a class ring, some foreign coins, nuts and bolts, colorful cancelled stamps, some baby teeth, and her father's Sunday School attendance pin with thirteen bars attached to it that each represented a year of perfect attendance. Now she knew what he treasured. Gently, she closed the lid.

Sitting next to the jewelry box was her mother's dusting powder with a fluffy pink puff inside. She recognized the smell of honeysuckle, her mother's favorite scent. Pulling up her shirt, she powdered herself liberally, leaving a snowy blanket of powder on the floor and dresser.

As she was about to leave, she noticed a half-finished dress her mother was making for her sister Lenore draped over the sewing machine that was tucked into another corner of the room. She held it up to herself. It was beautiful and sophisticated, just like Lenore. Cassie idolized her. She felt so awkward and plain and stupid next to Lenore, even though Cassie would never admit that to her older sister, or anyone else for that matter.

Cassie put the dress back, turned out the light, and pulled the door shut on her way out. Seeing that dress had given her a great idea. Now was her chance to explore Lenore's room!

Actually, Lenore didn't have a bedroom. She, like Cassie and Christy, had a corner of the unfinished attic where she slept and kept all her things. But Lenore's corner had a curtain hung around it and no one was allowed to go behind it. During the middle of the night, when the moon cast shadows through the small attic window, Cassie took great comfort in knowing Lenore was just beyond that curtain.

"Lenore," Cassie would call in a loud whisper from beneath her covers. "There's a moose (or a monster, or a man, or "whatever") in my closet."

"It's just the shadow from your clothes, Cassie," Lenore would say with an impatient sigh from beyond the veil. "Now go to sleep." And Cassie usually would.

Checking out the picture window to make sure her mother wasn't back, Cassie hurried down the hall and opened the attic door. She gazed up the steep staircase, gathering her courage before she bounded up the stairs, two at a time. Her desire to go beyond the mysterious curtain, plus the adventure of exploring "her" house, overruling her usual fears.

The curtain to Lenore's sleeping area was a dingy ivory with loud pink flowers scattered here and there. It parted in the middle, and Cassie stepped through, holding her breath, her eyes tightly shut. When she opened them, expecting to see Paradise, all she saw was a rumpled bed, a cluttered dresser, and a clothes rack that held Lenore's sparse wardrobe. There were no satin sheets or mysterious beauty potions, just a few bottles of spray cologne, a couple stuffed animals, and some well-worn rag dolls.

Cassie poked through the dresser drawers and found some mildly interesting love letters from Lenore's boyfriend, Howard, but nothing else was worth a second look. What a disappointment!

Suddenly, she heard a car pull into the driveway. Her mother was back! On impulse, she grabbed one of the bottles of cologne and sprayed herself generously, then dashed back through the curtain and down the stairs.

Just as she reached the bottom step and closed the door behind her, she heard her mother and brothers come in the back door. She tiptoed quickly into the living room, slipped onto the sofa, and pulled the afghan up over her head while her mother put the boys down for a nap before coming to check on her.

"Cassie," she called softly as she tapped her on the shoulder. "Are you feeling any better?"

"Yes, mama, I guess I am," Cassie said as she sat up and rubbed her eyes.

"You didn't get into anything while I was gone, did you?" her mother asked suspiciously, her hands on her hips.

Cassie looked at her mother with amazement. How could she think such a thing? "Of course not, mama," she said sincerely, her teeth black from Oreo cookies, her face white with powder and the smell of honeysuckle and Lenore's cheap cologne filling the room.

"Cassie Marie Johnson," her mother replied, shaking her head in disbelief. "What am I going to do with you? Were you afraid to be home alone?"

"Nope," Cassie smiled proudly. "Me and the house got along just fine."

Coming Out of Her Shell

Most days Cassie could hardly wait to get to school.
She was a good student and had a natural curiosity.
Now that she could read fairly well, school was even
more fun. She had discovered she could explore the
world, and everything about it, through books, and the
more she read, the more she wanted to know.

Cassie was not shy at home at all, but at school it was
a different story. While she always participated and
tried to do her best, she did not feel as secure there,
so she was quieter. But lately, she noticed something
happening when she was asked to read out loud in
class. Cassie came out of her shell!

Everyone seemed to enjoy listening to her read. At
first, she wasn't even aware of it, she was just doing
what came naturally. But the teacher began calling on
her to read more often, and she was comfortable doing

it. She would become so caught up in what she was reading that she didn't notice her classmates' eyes on her as she stood at the front of the class.

Miss Edie, her new teacher, was a nice lady, but Cassie wasn't sure she would ever like her as much as her last teacher, Mrs. Cook. She looked funny. She had buck teeth, black glasses, straight dark hair with really short bangs, and always wore a white blouse, dark skirt, and old-lady shoes. Mrs. Cook, on the other hand, was young, blonde, very pretty and had an air of mystery about her. But Cassie could tell Miss Edie liked her; she called on her to read often, and always said "Good job" when she was done.

One day the class was doing arithmetic worksheets quietly at their seats, when Miss Edie called Cassie up to her desk.

"Cassie," she whispered. "I want you to go to the library and see Mrs. Pethyridge. Here's a hall pass." She handed Cassie a slip of paper, and sent her on her way.

Cassie's school was brand new, and had a beautiful library. Once a week her class had library time to pick out books to read. They weren't allowed to take the books home, but used them during quiet reading time at their desks. She was sure Miss Edie was sending her on an errand to pick up a new book for class.

Mrs. Pethyridge, the librarian, was the oldest person in the school. She reminded Cassie of her grandmother. She treated the books in her care as if they were made of gold, and kept the library, and the children who visited there every day, in perfect order.

Cassie walked as silently as she could up to the check-out desk where Mrs. Pethyridge was sorting through books.

"Hello, Mrs. Pethyridge," she whispered. "Miss Edie sent me to see you."

"Ah, yes. Cassie Marie Johnson," Mrs. Pethyridge said pleasantly. "You must be my new helper."

Cassie caught her breath as she continued.

"Miss Edie tells me you are the best reader in her class, and one of her best students in every subject. So, she has chosen you to come down on Tuesdays and Thursdays to help me for an hour or so."

No one else was in the library as Mrs. Pethyridge took Cassie around and showed her how to put returned books back on the shelves by the author's last name. When that was done, she let Cassie practice using the date stamp and showed her how to file the check-out cards so she could keep track of which books were overdue. The next time Cassie came she would be helping students find books, checking them out, and then putting the books away that were returned.

By the time she got back to class, it was time for morning break, and Miss Edie had decided they could play eraser tag. Everyone had an equal chance to play because they took turns by rows, but whoever was able to keep the eraser on their head without being tagged as they raced around the room and back to Miss Edie's desk, could continue to play. It was hard for the class to contain their excitement, but the rules were clear; if you got out of your seat or made a lot of noise during the game, you lost your turn.

One after another of her classmates tried and failed to keep the chalkboard eraser balanced on their head, until finally it was Cassie's turn. She had been watching closely as they played, and had come up with a plan. The secret, she had decided, was to not move your head once the eraser was on top of it. That meant no laughing, no looking at anyone or anything, and just moving your lower body as fast as you could while you stared straight ahead.

She dashed to the front of the room, situated the eraser firmly on her head, glanced briefly at Angela who was her "chaser", and then let her long legs take over as she walked briskly around the room. Angela couldn't keep up with her, and dropped her eraser about halfway through when she got frustrated and turned her head to make eye contact with her best friend, Joyce.

Cassie won eraser tag, and returned to her desk, content with herself.

Just before dismissal time, Miss Edie announced that the school was going to be doing a play. Auditions would be held in the auditorium after school the next Thursday for anyone who wanted to try out for a part. Cassie wanted to try out in the worst way, but the knot in her stomach was telling her otherwise. She had never been on a stage before.

As she was gathering up her things to go home, Miss Edie again called her up to her desk. Twice in one day! Now what did she want, she wondered.

Taking her aside, Miss Edie sat on one of the desktops and had Cassie sit opposite her. The rest of the class filed out, and they were alone.

"How did it go with Mrs. Pethyridge?" Miss Edie asked.

"I liked it," Cassie said simply. It never entered her mind to say thank you, or to even ask why she had been chosen for such an honor.

"Good. I'm glad," Miss Edie replied. "There's something else I'd like you to do," she continued. "I want you to try out for the play next week. You are a natural performer, Cassie, and I think you would be perfect for the role of Mrs. Pigglewiggle."

Before she could say, "No way!", Miss Edie stood up and moved toward the door. "Just think about it," she said. "I know you're a little shy, but I think you can do this."

Mrs. Pigglewiggle was one of Cassie's favorite characters. She loved to read about her curious ways of curing naughty children of their bad behavior. For the next week she thought, and thought about what Miss Edie had said. One part of her tummy was scared to death, the other was excited and happy.

She would love to pretend to be Mrs. Pigglewiggle, but she had never acted before. What should she do? What if she tried out, and didn't get the part? She would be so upset. What if she got the part and then forgot her lines? She didn't want to make a fool of herself. But then, what if she did get the part and she didn't forget her lines? That would be so much fun, and she would be so proud of herself. That happy thought quickly faded when she remembered The Stage. How could she get up in front of all those people?

Working in the library helped take her mind off the play. Mrs. Pethyridge was so nice, and the other children were jealous of her. Cassie began to feel more confident. She won at eraser tag two more times, and she noticed that a couple of her classmates had figured out her strategy. The competition grew fiercer, and she had to work harder to stay ahead. Cassie found herself relaxing each day as the auditions drew nearer. "So, what if I don't try out," she began to reason to herself. "I still have the library, and eraser tag."

When Thursday arrived, she ate her cold cereal and drank her juice in silence, and Mrs. Johnson could tell something was bothering her.

"What's wrong, Cassie," she questioned. "Do you feel all right?"

For some reason, Cassie was thinking about eraser tag: Keep your head up, look straight ahead, don't look around. If she could do it in the classroom in front of all her classmates with an eraser on her head, she figured, maybe she could do it on The Stage.

"No, I'm fine, Momma," she replied brightly, her mind finally made up. "But I'll be late coming home after school. I'm going to try out for a play."

A Change of Heart

Cassie raced into the house.

"Mom, Mom," she called, "Howard is sitting in the middle of your flower bed again."

Mrs. Johnson was coming up the cellar stairs with a basket full of laundry. She dropped the clothes basket on the kitchen table, grabbed the fly swatter from under the sink, and headed for the front door, waddling as fast as she could.

"That blasted dog!" she snapped as the door slammed shut behind her.

Sure enough, sitting nonchalantly in the very midst of Mrs. Johnson's precious petunias, was Howard, the Basset Hound. His droopy eyes followed Mrs. Johnson with mild interest as she approached him.

"Get out of my petunias, you stupid dog!" she scolded, as she smacked him lightly on the rump with the fly swatter.

Howard just looked at her and wagged his tail, causing even more damage. Mrs. Johnson reached down, grabbed his collar, dragged him to his feet and pulled him out of the flower bed and onto the grass where he collapsed again, offering her his stomach to scratch. His tongue was hanging out, his long ears were askew, and his droopy skin sagged down loosely around him in cascading folds.

"Now go home," Mrs. Johnson commanded sternly, pointing in the right direction.

Ever so slowly, Howard rolled over, got to his feet and plodded toward his own home, looking sadly back at Mrs. Johnson.

Cassie helped her mother reinforce the plants that could be saved by packing soil around them, and together they pinched off the crushed blooms.

"I thought you were going to Ricky's house," her mother said as she dusted dirt from her hands.

"I was," Cassie replied, "But when I saw Howard, I came back."

"Thanks, hon. Why don't you go now while you still have time before dinner. I'll finish up here," her mother said, smiling.

"Okay. See you later." Cassie ran down the street toward her friend Ricky's house, passing Howard on the way.

A Change of Heart

She only had a couple blocks to go, but soon slowed to a walk. About halfway there, she spotted Patrick Shaw playing on one of the dirt piles made by the construction crews that were building new homes at the far end of the housing development where Cassie lived. As she walked by, she blushed.

Patrick was The Big Man at school. All the girls liked him because he was funny, and cute. Cassie wondered if he had seen her when a small stone whizzed by her and hit the curbstone. Soon, more gravel and dirt clods followed. He had seen her!

"Patrick, cut that out!" Cassie yelled, half mad and half happy. She knew if Patrick picked on a girl, it meant he liked her. She couldn't believe her luck, or her next thought: Maybe Patrick would even kiss her someday!

Cassie ran until she was out of range of the sailing debris, breathless but excited about the possibility that Patrick might like her. She couldn't wait to tell Ricky the news!

Ricky wasn't a boyfriend, like Patrick. He was just a friend who happened to be a boy. He was shy, a little on the chubby side, and Cassie didn't think he would ever throw anything at a girl. He was too polite.

When she arrived at his house, she rang the bell and waited for Ricky to appear.

"Hi, Cassie," he said with a grin as he opened the door for her to come in.

"Hi, Ricky. Hi, Mrs. Duthe!" Cassie called in to Ricky's mother.

Mrs. Duthe looked up from peeling potatoes, "Hi Cassie. Come on in and I'll get you two a snack."

Cassie and Ricky sat down at the kitchen table.

"Guess what, Ricky?" Cassie blurted out as soon as they were seated, "I think Patrick likes me! Yesterday he was chasing me on the playground, and on the way over here, he was throwing stuff at me!"

"Oh, that's nice," Ricky replied, then changed the subject, "Can you say all the Presidents in order yet?"

"Of course, I can," Cassie retorted, her mouth full of cookie. "Let's see, now. Washington, Adams, Jefferson, Madison, Monroe..." and she rattled them all off without a pause and in perfect order.

"Wow!" Ricky said reverently, "I don't even think I can say them that fast. Can you say them backwards?"

"Nah, not yet. But I'm working on it. Can you?" she inquired.

"Almost. I think I can do it by next week. Wanna bet?"

"Sure, what do you wanna bet?"

"How about my piece of granite for your arrowhead?"

"Okay, you're on," Cassie agreed and they shook on it.

They chattered on while they finished their snack, quizzing each other about the Presidents. Together, their knowledge was pretty impressive. They knew all the presidents' first names, who had been assassinated, and even trivia such as William Harrison had only been President for one month, Andrew Johnson was impeached, and the Teddy Bear was named after Teddy Roosevelt.

When their cookies were gone and they were done talking about the Presidents, they left the kitchen and moved into the living room. It was time to play some songs on the piano.

Ricky opened one of his songbooks to "Over the Rainbow" and he played the left-hand score while Cassie played the right. They worked on the piece over and over again until they could play and sing it together at the same time, very slowly.

Mrs. Duthe interrupted them just as they were ready to start a new piece. "Hey kids, that sounded great, but it's supper time and Cassie needs to head home."

Ricky walked Cassie to the back door.

"Well, I'll see you at school tomorrow, Ricky," Cassie said.

"Sure," said Ricky, and then, without any warning, he planted a very sloppy kiss on Cassie's cheek!

Equally without warning, Cassie found herself giving him a quick peck on the cheek in return, then she mumbled good-bye and left. Her face was burning, and her stomach was in a knot, but she felt very giddy and a little confused.

Cassie walked home slowly, weighing the afternoon's events in her mind. The street and dirt piles were deserted. Everyone was eating supper, so she quickened her pace.

As she neared home, she saw Lenore's boyfriend, Howard, pull up in front of the house. Cassie wondered if he had ever kissed Lenore.

Running up the back stairs, she slipped into the kitchen, hoping they hadn't begun eating without her. They were just sitting down, ready to say grace.

"Howard's out front," she announced as she took her seat.

Immediately, Mrs. Johnson grabbed a newspaper, rolled it up, and headed for the front door.

"That blasted dog!" she hollered, waving the newspaper, fire in her eyes.

"What is she doing?" Cassie thought to herself. Then she and everyone else at the table started laughing as a very embarrassed Mrs. Johnson walked back into the kitchen, followed by Lenore's very bewildered boyfriend.

"Hi, everybody," he said to the laughing family, "You ready, Lenore?"

Lenore pushed back from the table, ran into the hallway to grab her purse, and joined Howard at the door. He draped his arm casually around her shoulder and guided her toward the front door.

"I'll grab something to eat out, Ma" said Lenore as they left.

Cassie could hear Howard ask Lenore, "What's so funny?" and Lenore just put her arm around his waist and replied, "I'll tell you in the car."

Cassie wiped the tears of laughter from her eyes and filled her plate with lukewarm food. "Who knows," she thought to herself dreamily, "Maybe someday, that will be me and......"

She paused as she thought for a minute about who she would like her boyfriend to be.

"Ricky" she blurted out loud, startling her family.

And with that decision made, she turned her attention to her mashed potatoes and gravy.

A Matter of Honor

The door slammed behind Cassie as she jumped all four stairs to land with a splash on the wet driveway. She paused automatically to pull up her socks and tried in vain to hide the plastic bread bags her mother insisted she wear inside her rain boots because they had cracks in the back seams. It was cold and damp, but the house was noisy and cramped with five children stuck inside because of the nasty weather. She was glad to be outside, away from the chaos.

It was Saturday, and the morning had gone by quickly while everyone was watching cartoons, but once the TV was turned off, she was put in charge of keeping an eye on her little brother Tommy. He insisted on taking his clothes off and streaking around the house stark naked.

After fighting to put his clothes back on several times as he squirmed and shrieked, Lenore relieved her of her babysitting duties, but not without lecturing her first on how to do a better job. Her mother agreed with Lenore, and being very pregnant, she was downright grouchy, so her scolding was particularly unpleasant. With red cheeks and her temper barely in check, Cassie had escaped to the quiet relief of the outdoors.

She walked slowly down the driveway, turned onto the sidewalk and was a couple houses away when she heard a door slam behind her. She turned around just in time to see Christy emerge from their house, walk cautiously down the stairs, and look around, searching for something.

"Oh, bother," she groaned to herself. "I bet Christy is looking for me!"

With that thought, she ran down the street and hid between two houses until Christy gave up her search for her older sister and went back into the house. It wasn't that Cassie didn't care about Christy; she just considered her a drag. She was so klutzy Cassie spent half their time together waiting for her to catch up, or picking Christy up off the ground. She was always tripping over her own two feet!

Cassie continued down the street until she was sure she was out of sight of the house, then she headed for Mrs. Miller's trailer, one of several mobile homes that occupied the far corner of their street.

Mrs. Miller had a Siamese cat named Tinker that Cassie walked for her whenever the weather was bad. The cold made Mrs. Miller ache all over, and the heat made her feel faint, so Cassie walked Tinker frequently, and received a nickel each time she did.

Mrs. Miller was glad to see Cassie, but Tinker was not. As soon as the cat saw her, she hid under the sofa, and it took Mrs. Miller and Cassie at least fifteen minutes to pull her out and get her harness and leash on. Tinker glowered at both of them with her blue eyes while Mrs. Miller tried to assure her that cold, damp air is good for cats. Tinker obviously was not convinced that going out was in her best interest, and protested loudly when Cassie pulled her out the door and down the stairs. Once they were outside, though, Tinker relaxed and led the way.

Cassie was glad when Tinker headed for The Woods. The trees would offer some protection from the rain and they both enjoyed exploring there. They picked their way through the damp leaves that covered the ground, stopping occasionally so Tinker could investigate a hole or listen to a sound only she could hear. When they left The Woods to head back to the trailer, Cassie spotted her friend Billy across the street in the middle of the Pollywog Pond.

Curious, she and Tinker crossed the street to see what Billy was up to. He was testing new hip boots and held up a jar filled with pollywogs, a huge grin on his face.

Cassie brushed aside some leaves and sat down on the damp ground to watch for a while, but soon began to shiver. Tinker began to yowl, so she stood up, brushed herself off, waved goodbye to Billy, and headed once again toward Mrs. Miller's trailer. Realizing where they were going, Tinker began to pull on the harness, dragging Cassie in her haste to get back to her warm abode.

Mrs. Miller pressed a nickel into Cassie's cold palm and they made arrangements for her to walk Tinker the next day. Cassie stuffed the nickel in her coat pocket and bolted out the door, narrowly escaping one of Mrs. Miller's awkward hugs.

Cassie's behind was cold and wet from sitting on the ground, her nose was starting to drip, and the drizzle was getting heavier, so she decided to go home. As the house came into view, she could see her mother's pregnant frame filling the picture window as Mrs. Johnson checked on her whereabouts.

Cassie waved, and her mother waved back, motioning her to come home to eat. She felt much better after her time outdoors, despite being chilled, and walked faster so she could rejoin the family for a hot lunch. Her mother was a good cook, and she knew they were having grilled cheese sandwiches and homemade tomato soup; one of her favorite meals.

Suddenly, she heard footsteps behind her. Turning around she saw Butchie walking quickly to catch up to her. He was at least a head taller than Cassie, and all the kids in the neighborhood were intimidated by his size. She cringed at the mere sight of him, so she lowered her head against the rain and picked up her pace as she tried to ignore him.

"Hey, Johnson," he said in a loud voice as he gained on her. "Was that 'thing' in the window your mother? She's so FAT she couldn't hide behind those curtains if she tried!" And he laughed at his own very unfunny joke.

Cassie looked up and down the street to see if anyone had heard his remark. No one was in sight. She felt her face flush as she clenched her fists at her sides. She turned and stared up at Butchie's laughing face. Then, without thinking, she flung herself at him, catching him by surprise and knocking him to the ground.

"Why, YOU!" she yelled. "She's not fat, she's PREGNANT!!" She sat on his chest, flinging soggy leaves and whatever else she could grab into his face. Then she stood up, gave him a quick, hard kick in the leg and raced for the house while he tried to get up.

Her mother met Cassie at the back door with a towel and sent her directly to the cellar to take off her wet clothes. When she came back upstairs, she wanted to tell her mother what had happened with Butchie, and how she had defended her honor, but Mrs. Johnson was busy trying to settle everyone around the table for lunch. It didn't seem like the right time to talk about it, so she went to her room to change into dry clothes.

Her stomach was growling by the time she returned. She had decided not to tell her family about the fight with Butchie. They probably wouldn't believe her anyway.

"Besides," she thought to herself with a touch of pride. "Butchie knows what happened, and that's all that counts." So, she gave Christy's hair a quick, friendly yank as she walked past her to her seat, and sat down to enjoy her own private victory feast.

The Best Gift

Cassie and Christy were deliberately walking as slowly as they could toward school, kicking loose cinders along the path as the other children walked past them. Then Cassie began walking backwards, as she tried to catch sight of the family car turning onto the street. The new baby was coming home!

It had been five days since their new brother had been born, and they couldn't wait to see him. When they left for school that morning, their father promised them their mother and baby Timmy would be home by the time they came home for their lunch break. Both girls had been disappointed to find Lenore making sandwiches for them when they arrived home at noon.

Lenore had been in charge of the house since the baby had been born, and Cassie could hardly wait for her mother to get back home. Lenore was so bossy! She was constantly yelling at Cassie to "keep the house clean for your mother", or "stop picking on Christy", or "eat what's put in front of you for pity's sake".

Cassie's mother said the same things, but for some reason it seemed all right for a mother to say bossy things. It was not all right coming from a big sister.

After lunch, Cassie had begged Lenore to let her stay home to wait for the baby to arrive rather than go back to school for the afternoon session.

"Please, Lenore," she pleaded, "I'm positively positive that Mama wouldn't mind it if I'm a little late for school, and Miss Edie will understand."

"No!" Lenore said sharply. "I want everything just right when they get home. Now go to school."

Cassie had stormed out of the house with Christy close behind and headed toward the school at the end of the street.

Now, as she continued walking backwards with Christy as her eyes, they were alone on the cinder path; everyone else was already back in school. Just as they reached the crosswalk to the schoolyard, Cassie saw their station wagon turn the corner at the far end of the street.

"Christy! There they are!" she squealed. "I'm going back home. Come on, let's go!"

Christy shook her head. "I don't want to get into trouble," she replied.

"Well, I don't care!" Cassie called over her shoulder as she ran toward home while Christy continued on her way back to class.

Cassie was careful as she ran along the cinder path toward home. She didn't want to trip and chance getting a knee full of cinder cuts. By the time she reached the concrete portion of the sidewalk, she had to stop to catch her breath. She could see the neighbors gathering around the car to admire the baby. The thought of seeing her new brother renewed her energy, and once more she broke into a run.

When she reached the driveway, Lenore was the first one to see her.

"Cassie, what are you doing here?" she asked in a threatening whisper.

Cassie ignored her now that her mother was home. She walked past Lenore and around the car until she was standing next to Mrs. Johnson who was sitting half in and half out of the car, gently holding the blanket back from Timmy's face so the neighbor ladies could see him.

Cassie was overwhelmed. The ladies were "oohing" and "aahing" their approval of the baby, while questions and comments whirled around Mrs. Johnson: "How much did he weigh? He looks just like Jeffrey! How are you feeling? I think he looks just like his father! What's his middle name? I don't think he looks like any of the other kids." Her mother just listened, looking tired but happy.

Cassie continued to gaze at the tiny bundle, grinning so hard her ears hurt. He was the most beautiful, most wonderful baby in the whole wide world!

Cassie's father had been unloading the car, taking the suitcase and baby supplies into the house. By the time he was done, the neighbors had begun to leave, so he took the baby from Mrs. Johnson so she could get to her feet, and then guided her up the steps and into the house. Cassie and Lenore followed them, exchanging dark glances.

Once the baby was tucked into the crib in her parents' bedroom, and Mrs. Johnson was settled in the kitchen with a hot cup of her favorite tea, her mother addressed Cassie.

"I know you're excited about the baby, Cassie," she said. "But you've got to go to school." Then, seeing the disappointment on Cassie's face, she added, "The baby will still be here when you get home."

Cassie waited silently while her mother wrote her a tardy excuse before she walked slowly back to school.

All afternoon she daydreamed about the baby. "I wonder if I'll get to hold him when I get home," she mused. "Maybe Momma will let me feed him. And maybe," she thought excitedly, "she'll even let me change his diaper!"

When she did get home from school, her hopes of holding the baby disappeared.

The house was bustling with people and activity. Mrs. Larson was there with a casserole for dinner. Mrs. Young and Mrs. Scotland had brought gifts over for the baby, and Mr. and Mrs. Brown had returned Jeffrey and Tommy who had been staying with them while Mrs. Johnson was in the hospital. Cassie's mother was sitting next to the bassinet in the living room opening gifts, while Tommy sat on her lap. Timmy was sound asleep, despite the noise, totally unaware he was the center of attention.

Cassie resigned herself to peeking at the cards and gifts, and absorbing the excitement as it flowed around her.

It was suppertime before things began to calm down. Mrs. Larson's casserole was good, but Cassie was tired of casseroles. The ladies from church had been bringing in supper for them all week, a different casserole each night. Cassie was glad her mother was home. She wanted things to get back to normal; normal food, a normal routine, even normal scoldings.

Every one was sent to bed early that evening so mother and baby could get some much-needed rest. Cassie lay in bed, thinking. She had noticed that everyone who had come to visit had brought the baby a gift. Even Christy had brought her mother a bouquet of last-of-the-season marigolds and some damp orange and yellow leaves.

Cassie didn't have any money to buy a gift, so what could she give to her mother and little Timmy? She thought, and thought, and finally, fell asleep.

The next morning was Saturday, and it was customary for her father to buy doughnuts and make eggs, pancakes and bacon. Cassie didn't like pancakes or bacon, but she ate three cream-filled doughnuts and some scrambled eggs before she slipped out the back door with a mason jar. She went around to the side of the house to the water spigot, filled the mason jar with water, and then headed for the Field. She had thought of a gift for her mother and baby brother.

At the far end of the field, beyond the Pussy Willow Bush, was an embankment that had a strip of rich, red clay running through it. Her mother always complained about the mess it made when it was tracked into the house, but today Cassie had thought of a good use for it.

Settling herself at the foot of the embankment on a patch of dry, yellow grass, she dug her fingernails into the clay, scooping out several stiff chunks. It wasn't soft and pliable like the clay at school, so taking her jar of water she began to wet it down, making it easier to mold.

It was chilly out, and as she worked, her fingers began to get stiff, but she was so absorbed in her creation she ignored both the stiffness and her red, drippy nose.

Cassie worked a long time, molding and smoothing, adding layer upon layer, using a popsicle stick to help shape her gift. Finally, it was done, and she slowly got to her feet. Her left foot was asleep, so she hobbled home, gingerly holding the damp clay in her cupped hands.

When she arrived, she had a hard time working her way in through the back door without denting her creation. Tiptoeing through the kitchen and past the living room where everyone was still watching cartoons, she knocked on her mother's bedroom door with her elbow.

"Who is it?" her mother's muffled voice responded.

"It's me, Momma," Cassie answered softly. "Can I come in?"

"All right," her mother replied. "But just for a minute."

Cassie nudged the door open with her shoulder and then closed it behind her with her fanny. The room was dark and quiet. Timmy was lying on his back on the bed next to his mother, wide awake.

"I have something for you and Timmy," Cassie said self-consciously. She held out both hands, and there, resting on her clay-caked palms, was a tiny cradle. An even tinier baby was nestled inside, covered by a thin clay blanket, with sleeping eyes and a smile thumbnail-etched on his face.

Cassie placed the cradle in her mother's outstretched hand and smiled as she watched her mother examine the detail and then gently rock it back and forth, ignoring the damp clay that was dripping onto her palm.

"It's lovely, Cassie," she finally said. "Let's put it on the dresser to dry." She got up off the bed and carefully placed the cradle on top of the dresser.

"Why don't you go wash your hands and you can hold the baby," her mother suggested.

Cassie raced across the hall to the bathroom, scraped the clay off her hands and scrubbed them with soap and hot water so they would be clean and warm. When she returned, her mother was waiting for her. She had Cassie sit on the edge of the bed before she placed little Timmy in the crook of her arm.

"Make sure you support his neck," Mrs. Johnson cautioned. Cassie looked into the bluish-gray eyes for a long time, and put her cheek against Timmy's soft one. He smelled wonderfully of baby powder and sweet, clean clothes, and his fine wisp of hair was softer than kittens' fur. Cassie sighed and brushed his cheek lightly with her lips.

Her mother stood, quietly watching. "I really like the cradle," she finally said. "You did an excellent job on it. It's one of the best gifts Timmy and I have received."

"Thank you," Cassie responded automatically, without taking her eyes off her baby brother. She was glad her mother liked the cradle, but she knew deep down that she was holding the very best gift of all in her arms.

The Corner to the World

As long as she could remember, Cassie's world had always been the same. Some things, she was sure, would never change, while other things would continue to change, just as they always had. She liked her everyday life with its mix of familiar sameness and normal changes.

For her, the small green house with the fenced yard and the clothesline where her mother hung laundry every morning, no matter what the weather, would always be the center of her universe. She rarely ventured beyond that Center, or her neighborhood, with the marshy fields and meadows that were slowly being overtaken by rows of frame houses. Together, they were more than just a place to play and explore. Her House, The Woods, The Pollywog Pond, and The Field were her security blanket, and her friends. She could count on her little world remaining the same.

Cassie also knew her family would always be there for her, and she was comfortable with each one of them. She knew she could count on Lenore to be bossy, Christy to be a pest, and Jeffrey to be a pain in the neck. Tommy was still too young to be anything but cute, but she had noticed he was acting less like a toddler, and more like a terrible-two-year-old. Baby Timmy's addition to the family was a good change, she decided, even if it meant sharing her parents with yet another child. She knew they would adjust in time.

Growing up was another change Cassie expected and looked forward to. She knew her shoes would get too tight, and her arms and legs would get longer, but lately, something else was changing, too, and Cassie was having a hard time figuring out what it was. Her father said she was getting "too big for her britches," Lenore insisted she was just being "as bratty as ever", but her mother simply believed she was "trying her wings." Cassie only knew she was seeing things in a different light, experiencing new thoughts and feelings, and doing things she never would have thought of doing before.

A few days after Timmy's homecoming, Cassie was walking down the street when she remembered something she had heard in Sunday School class the week before. She was sure her teacher, Mrs. Belmont, had told the whole class that if you prayed for something and truly believed, God would give you the answer to your prayer.

Cassie said her prayers almost every night, but she had never thought too much about them until now. She wondered what would happen if she tested what her teacher had said.

At the time Cassie had this unusual thought, she was at the end of her street, across from the trailer park, at the furthest point she was allowed to wander away from home. Across the street, around The Corner and down a few buildings, was Wolney's Stop 'n Shop. Just thinking about all the wonderful things they sold there made her thirsty for an orange soda. It seemed like the perfect thing to pray for!

She also remembered hearing that God can read your thoughts, so in her mind, but with her eyes tightly closed, she prayed, very sincerely: "Dear God, I really and truly do believe that You can give me an orange soda, if you would, please, and I am really thirsty, and to prove to you that I believe, I am going to go home right now and drink my orange soda." Then, remembering her father's suppertime prayers, she quickly added: "In Jesus' name, Amen."

With that done, she turned and raced past the ten houses that stood between her and the refrigerator, darted up her driveway, and slammed the back door as she flew into the house. She went directly to the kitchen, opened the refrigerator door, and reached in for her orange soda.

It wasn't there! Convinced it must be in there, somewhere, she rummaged through the whole refrigerator, but came up empty-handed.

"Cassie Marie Johnson!" her mother interrupted. "What are you doing, letting all the cold air out of the fridge?"

Cassie knew her mother wouldn't understand, or, at best, she would laugh at her and say she was "cute," so she mumbled something about "wanting an ice cube" and went back outside to think some more.

As she sat on the back steps, wondering what was wrong with her prayer, a new thought suddenly dawned on her!

The orange soda, the questions that kept invading her mind about anything and everything, the self-consciousness, the changing that she felt but didn't know how to explain...... She knew what was happening! SHE was changing inside her head! She was asking HERSELF questions, and finding her own answers, or at least trying to. She wasn't content to rely on her mother, her father, or even Lenore to explain things to her. Cassie was finding out about herself and her world, all by herself!

Her father interrupted her revelation when he drove in the driveway.

"Hi, dad," Cassie said cheerfully. Then, feeling very proud and bold, she added, "Can I have a quarter to walk up to Wolney's and get an orange soda?"

Mr. Johnson studied her for a minute, then reached into his pocket, pulled out his loose change, and handed her a quarter.

"Just make sure you look both ways before you cross the street," he said.

As Cassie skipped down the street, then obediently looked both ways before crossing the street and turning The Corner for the first time by herself, she noticed every little detail along the way. She knew this new path would become familiar, even comfortable, over time, and she welcomed the change in her normal routine.

She was beginning to enjoy the change in herself, too, now that she understood what it meant. She was glad she was growing up, inside and out, becoming more independent, and thinking for herself. It was a good thing. But she was also sure the small green house with the fenced-in yard and the clothesline where her mother hung laundry every morning, no matter what the weather was like, would still be the center of her universe for many years to come.

The End

Janet Karr Palmer was born and raised in Western New York and is the second oldest of eight children. Her inspiration for Cassie is based on her preteen years growing up in her large family in Niagara Falls, NY in the early 60's.

After raising her own five children, she is now retired, and along with her husband, Mark, and youngest brother Timothy, lives in The Villages, Florida.

She still enjoys her lifelong loves of nature, writing, learning, exploring, and connecting with people of all ages. She continues to wonder what she will be when she grows up, but in the meantime is keeping busy bowling, golfing, volunteering as an editor/writer for a monthly newspaper, teaching Bible studies, doing crafts, walking the dogs, learning how to dance in public, visiting her grandkids, and eating out as often as possible. As a grown up Cassie, she would advise others that: "We don't stop playing because we grow old; we grow old because we stop playing."
George Bernard Shaw